A Husband and Wife Are One Satan

"Literature's best magic trick may be to entice us to enter lives/countries/ cultures we otherwise have no access to—in this case contemporary Kazakhstan—whereupon we immediately recognize the Kazakh version of ourselves. In these poignant, good-humored, heart-breaking, and well-crafted stories, fiery women attempt to hold their own against toxic masculinity, tribalism dies hard, if at all, and the human heart most wants something to believe in."
–**Pam Houston**, author of *Deep Creek: Finding Hope in the High Country*

"In this beautiful, solemn collection of stories, Jeff Fearnside has employed Chekovian precision to bring to life a place of transition and turmoil, its people holding to the traditions of old as a new world forms around them in all its damning weight and splendor, each tale intimate and soulful and profound. This book is moving and thoughtful, delivering insights into love and war and family and country with the depth and sincerity found only in the best of literature."
–**Alan Heathcock**, author of *VOLT* and *40*

"Jeff Fearnside's *A Husband and Wife Are One Satan* captures everyday life in the Republic of Kazakhstan, a place that feels darkly different and hilariously familiar. Rich with memorable characters and stark beauty, Fearnside's stories are deft in their crafting, and often they pivot from funny to bleak in a flash. The truths here, of what it is to be a human being, are universal and a joy to read."
–**Margaret Malone**, author of *People Like You*

"Jeff Fearnside is a writer of great range, complication, and empathy. Rooted in place, awash in history, often cornered by cultural expectations, his characters are nevertheless living, breathing human beings, possessed of their own desires and dreams, their own failures and heroisms. I only wish there were more of these stories."
–**Joe Wilkins**, author of *Fall Back Down When I Die* and *The Mountain and the Fathers*

A Husband and Wife Are One Satan

stories by

Jeff Fearnside

A Husband and Wife Are One Satan

Print ISBN: 978-1-949039-27-6
E-book ISBN: 978-1-949039-28-3

Orison Books
PO Box 8385
Asheville, NC 28814
www.orisonbooks.com

Distributed to the trade by Itasca Books
1-800-901-3480 / orders@itascabooks.com

Cover image courtesy of Shutterstock.

Manufactured in the U.S.A.

ORISON
BOOKS

CONTENTS

We grow out of earth, out of all its impurities, and everything that exists in the earth exists in us . . . . From our ugliness grows the soul of the world.

–Andrei Platonov

Accomplices to a Tradition

I'd almost made it home to my microregion when I was flagged down. I stopped, grabbed my registration papers from the glove compartment—and some money from the ashtray in case I needed to pay a bribe—but before I could get out of the car, the policeman was already standing at my door.

"I need a ride," he said.

I'd seen him at this corner many times before. If I refused him now, he would likely make my life difficult later. So even though my wife was waiting for me, I motioned for him to get in. I was guessing he wanted to buy some vodka and then have me take him home.

"Go to the next street and turn right," he said from the back seat. I did, but as we were passing the store that sold liquor, he didn't say anything more.

"Here?" I asked.

"Farther. I'll tell you when to stop."

He asked for a cigarette, and we both lit up. He was a strong-looking ethnic Kazakh, though not as strong as me, about my age. I was twenty-five then, newly married, and though it was a beautiful summer evening, I wanted to get home to my wife. But we just drove along in silence, him pointing directions, until we were nearly out of town. Now I began getting worried. Was he taking me somewhere out of the way so he could shake me down for a really big bribe? Then why did he stop me, just another young guy in an old Lada? I'd only just started working as a guard at one of the tourist hotels in town, and my wife and I were still living with my parents.

"There," he said finally, pointing to three people standing by the last bus stop at the end of town, where the steppe began. "I need to pick up my friends."

I stopped, and they all got in, a young man with a bag and a girl holding roses joining the policeman in back, another girl sitting up front with me. They all looked like ethnic Kazakhs, the new guy also about twenty-five, the girls about eighteen.

"Do you know the lake?" the policeman asked. I nodded. "Good. That's where we're going."

I looked at my gas gauge. The policeman must have been looking over my shoulder because he said, "You have enough." He then said something to his friends in Kazakh, and they all laughed.

I was beginning to wish he had just asked me for a bribe and let me go. This was going to end up costing me a lot, I figured, but I didn't know what else to do. So I just started driving and tried to enjoy myself, lighting up another cigarette. It was hot out on the steppe, but still very beautiful. I would have enjoyed it more if I hadn't been driving but drinking a little vodka instead. The guy with the bag must have been thinking the same, because after about five minutes he pulled out a bottle. They passed it around to everyone and then offered it to me. Though I wanted some, I said that I had a long way to go. The policeman seemed to think this was funny.

"Good, good! You shouldn't drink while you drive. It's against the law."

When talking directly to me like that, they spoke in Russian, but with each other they spoke in Kazakh. I've lived in Kazakhstan all my life, but I was never able to learn any more Kazakh than what I picked up from friends at school, mostly slang. I could actually swear pretty good whenever I needed it in a fight. But I only understood a word here, a phrase there, of the conversation now going on in my car. It seems the men were close friends who'd known each other for years. The girls were, too, though they'd only known the men for a short time. Something about mutual acquaintances, a family connection. There was talk of "a party" and "swimming." Since it was Friday, I guessed they were planning on spending the weekend at the lake. They all seemed comfortable with each other, and they quickly finished off the bottle.

By now I knew all their names. Arman was the policeman, Nurken his friend. The woman sitting between them was Saparkul. She had the long, thick ponytail that many Kazakh girls wear before getting married, a dark mole on her cheek matching her dark eyes. I kept staring at her in the rearview mirror, though she never looked at me. Perizat was sitting up front. Both women were smartly dressed, short skirts, high heels, very modern. I could see that they had swimsuits on underneath their clothes.

"Brother, do you want to join us at the lake?" Arman asked.

"No, no, I can't. My wife's waiting for me at home."

"Who's in charge?" he cried, slapping me on the shoulder. "You or your wife?"

In the rearview mirror I saw Nurken smirking, but Perizat turned around and said, "The man may be the head, but the woman is the neck." Everyone howled at this, and Arman started arguing with her, comparing the intelligence of men and women. He thought he was winning, but while she'd probably only just finished her first year at one of the local universities, she was clearly better educated, from a good family, not a village girl. She and Saparkul both seemed this way. They didn't smoke, and they drank modestly, leaving most of the vodka for Arman and Nurken. The men held their alcohol well, hardly seemed drunk at all. I was actually beginning to like them, but they didn't seem the best match for these girls. I guessed they were all just looking for a little fun. I'm not sure exactly what the girls had been told, but whatever it was, they didn't seem to mind.

Nurken pulled out another bottle, and we continued driving through the evening. My wife wasn't going to be happy, but what could she do? Being taken for a ride by the police wasn't that uncommon. I wouldn't even have to lie this time.

As we approached the turnoff for the lake, Arman leaned over me and said quietly, "Turn left."

"But—" I began, but he squeezed my shoulder with one hand and pointed with the other. He was even stronger than I'd thought.

"You made a wrong turn," Saparkul said to me. When no one else said anything, including Perizat, I began to get a bad feeling.

"The lake is that way," she repeated. Still no one said a word.

Suddenly she began screaming. I didn't understand everything, but I understood enough.

"Stop the car! Stop the car!"

Now I knew why Arman had flagged me down. Saparkul was being "stolen." It was an old Kazakh tradition. It was also against the law. I thought of slamming on the brakes, but then what would I do? Arman was a policeman. He could accuse me of doing anything, and no judge would rule otherwise. I could've fought both men if I'd had to—I've fought more before—but they were strong and had been drinking, and we were in the middle of the devil's land. If I lost they'd just throw me to the side of the road, and who knows when I'd be found? I'd be helping no one then.

Saparkul tried to crawl over Arman and open the door, but he grabbed her around the waist and pulled her back. She began beating him on the head and neck, so he took hold of her arms. I was having a hard time staying on the road, turning to see what was happening and wondering if I should intervene.

"Keep driving," Arman said calmly. "To the village."

Saparkul began pleading with me in Russian.

"Please stop the car, please. You have to help me. I don't want to get married. I want to finish my education. I have a boyfriend in town. Please help me."

I almost slowed the car.

"You're hurting her," I said.

"He's not hurting her," Nurken said. "Everything is fine."

"She says she doesn't want to go."

"I said everything is fine. This is our tradition."

It was true. Often it was done with the girl's approval, a way for her poor young fiancé to avoid paying the bride price. Often it was done without the girl's approval or even her knowing it was going to happen. Saparkul was clearly in this second group. It was hard to say why Arman wanted her. Perhaps he truly loved her. Perhaps he just found her beautiful. But once the kerchief was tied around her head by his grandmother, the girl had no choice but to accept her fate; otherwise she'd bring shame to her family.

The village came into view through the shimmering heat rising from the steppe, like something from an ancient caravan scene. Why didn't I stop the car, or better yet, turn it around? All I know is that I was confused. Though bride stealing was against the law, it was tolerated then just as it is today. The only time a case could be formed against anyone was when the girl really caused a scene. Suppose Saparkul got this chance. What would happen to me? I was an accomplice to all this. After all, it was my car she was being stolen in. Arman would say I'd known about it from the beginning, maybe even helped plan it.

"This isn't right," I said.

Perizat moved for the first time since the turn.

"You don't understand," she said. "This is our *tradition*."

Saparkul began screaming at her friend in Kazakh. I knew the curse words. The men told me to mind my own business. They'd known lots of women who'd been stolen and learned to love their husbands. Arman's grandmother was one, he said. Perizat nodded in agreement, and without turning around, though she raised her voice, she said that Saparkul would get used to her new life and be happy.

We had arrived at the village. I felt like I was in a dream as Arman directed me down one narrow dirt lane and then another. I didn't need him to tell me which house to stop at. I saw the old grandmother standing in the doorway in her brightly colored housecoat, the kerchief in both hands. Several men stood in the yard, empty shot glasses between their fingers. Another man was butchering a sheep hung from a tree, while children played around the entrails. Arman and Nurken had to drag Saparkul from the car, prying her fingers from the doorframe. She began screaming again, her ponytail, now pulled loose, wild over her face and shoulders. I couldn't help but wonder whether she would keep that beautiful hair. Arman closed the door and leaned in through the open window.

"Thank you," he said.

I turned the car around and drove very slowly back to town.

Learning to Fly at the End of an Empire

To us then, in summer, our grandparents' dacha was the whole world—that small plot of land with the little country house Grandpa had built with his own hands, like a Kazakhstani man is supposed to, back when Brezhnev was still in charge. By the time I was a schoolgirl, the trees had grown tall and leafy, and it was a quiet oasis of coolness in the blazing desert heat. After the last bell had rung, my brother and I would stay for weeks at a time, sharing a room with Granny while Grandpa slept in a small room off the kitchen. Our parents slept outside on the raised tapchan whenever they came on weekends.

And like all Kazakhstani boys, then and now, it was important for my brother to show his "manhood." Yura was only half my ten years and small for his age; his little body looked as if it might be swallowed whole by the monstrous tentacles of the raspberry bushes. So to prove his bravery, he would wait until evening, when the backyard came alive under darkness, and then race alone down the path through the garden, past those brute bushes, the dark walnut trees, the tall outhouse and all the way to the vine-covered fence that marked the end of our share of communal property. Then, like Ulysses returning from far foreign lands, he would race back to Granny's open arms and Grandpa's slap on the shoulders, "Well done!" ringing in his ears, cigarette ash falling around his head like a laurel.

I can imagine how he felt: his little feet churning as fast as they could, the smell of wood smoke and earth and onions, every shadowy tomato plant a gnome with multiple bulbous noses, the nightly barking of dogs certainly the sound of wolves hunting for errant tasty snacks!

I can imagine how he felt because I used to fill his head with these images every night in our room before we went to sleep. We would pull the sheet over our heads, light a small candle, and huddle together like cave dwellers while I told stories to explain the world:

"Deep in the forest lives an old, old woman named Baba Yaga."

"What forest?" Yura interrupted. "In Russia?"

"No, here. In the mountains where Papa took us once." He nodded solemnly, and I continued. "Baba Yaga lives in a cabin, a special cabin. When you get lost in this forest—and you *always* get lost, no matter which path you take—you end up at the back of Baba Yaga's cabin. So you have to say, 'Cabin, cabin, turn your back to the forest and your front to me.' Then the cabin stands up and turns around."

"You mean it has legs?" Yura squeaked, as he always did when excited.

"Of course it has legs! It's magic. Now, when the house stands up and moves like that, it shakes things up. Pictures fall off the walls; the teakettle falls off the stove. This makes Baba Yaga angry. She comes marching out the door, saying, 'Who's there?' But she's also secretly happy because she wants lost children to find her."

"Why?"

"Because," and here I spoke slowly, "she wants to eat them."

Yura contemplated this with a lowered head and then looked up with wet, serious eyes. "Really?"

"Really. But not just any children. She likes little boys—" I pinched him in the stomach, and he jumped a bit, "and especially *bad* little boys. So you'd better be good, or else—"

The door to the room suddenly banged open, and a voice thundered, "What's going on in here?"

Yura and I both leaped up, and I spilled wax on my nightshirt while trying to hide the candle behind my back. "Baba Yaga, don't eat me!" he screamed.

Granny pulled the sheet away and rapped my brother's head with her knuckles.

"Baba Yaga? What are you talking about, you little bandit? You're supposed to be sleeping." She looked at me then, too. "Why aren't you both sleeping? Give me that." She held out her hand, and I immediately placed the candle there. "In five minutes the only sound I want to hear is the sound of two children sleeping. Understood?"

"Understood," we both said in unison.

She glared at us again, though in my memory now I can see gentle wrinkles of laughter around her eyes. "Baba Yaga!" she snorted before closing the door.

My brother, perhaps exhausted from his fright, fell asleep within minutes, but I lay awake and listened to the voices of the grownups as they discussed life over rounds of vodka and sour pickles. Mysterious words floated over the threshold from their world to ours: *glasnost, perestroika.* Something about being public or open, about rebuilding—but what exactly? I pretended to be asleep.

"Gorbachev is too soft," Grandpa was saying. "They tore the Berlin Wall down. Now the Baltics want to separate. What will be next? Glasnost," he muttered. "Perestroika."

"That you can call him soft shows that things are better now," my uncle said.

"You think standing in long lines for bread is better? Maybe a young man like you enjoys it, but it's not easy for us old folks."

"Sometimes sacrifices have to be made for progress."

"Sacrifices? What are you talking about, sacrifices? I made mine during the Great Patriotic War fighting the Nazi fascists."

"And I was clubbed in the head fighting our own fascists in Almaty."

"Akh," Grandpa said like he often did, followed by a creaking sound. I could easily imagine him leaning back on his chair and waving his hand as if swatting away a fly. "You were tricked into believing in a bad cause by decadent thugs and drug addicts. I've read the newspapers."

"I was there. I know what happened."

"Glasnost," Grandpa repeated bitterly. "Perestroika."

"Many people were killed," my uncle insisted, "workers and students, most of them women. Innocents."

It was only many years later, after my country's independence and my own womanhood, that he told me how it took the authorities all day to wash Brezhnev Square of blood.

*

In the morning our two older cousins taught my brother to fly. They pulled out the kitchen table, spread a thick blanket over it, and made Yura lie down upon it on his back.

"Will it hurt?" he asked.

"No," Pasha said. "Now close your eyes and listen closely to the magic words. Concentrate! If you open your eyes or don't concentrate on the words, it won't work."

Yura closed his eyes tightly. "Like this?"

"Tighter. Good. Now concentrate." Pasha and Anya then began chanting nonsense syllables in loud, theatrical voices: *abracadabra*, *akhalyai makhalyai*. While doing this, they carefully slid their hands under the blanket and Yura's back and legs.

"With these magic words you will fly!" Pasha was almost shouting now. "You will be like a bird! You will be like the wind!"

They slowly began lifting Yura from the table.

"I can feel something," he squeaked. "Am I flying?"

When he was level to my head, Yura suddenly threw open his eyes and yelled in terror. He thrashed in the arms that held him and fell with a resonant thump on the table.

"I told you not to open your eyes!" Pasha said sternly.

"I was flying! I was flying! Nadya, did you see me?" He rubbed his little behind. I nodded and made my eyes wide like dinner plates.

"Hurrah!" He jumped off the table and ran out the door, spreading his arms as if he were an airplane soaring all around the yard.

*

After lunch we played vybivaly. My brother and I stood together between our two cousins, each about four or five meters away. They had a rubber ball the size of a melon, and they took turns trying to hit us until we were both out.

"You can't hit me, you can't hit me," my brother taunted. "I can fly!" Pasha suddenly threw the ball, and Yura jumped, just clearing it. "See?"

When Anya missed me and Pasha got the ball back, he must have thought my brother would try to jump again; Pasha aimed high, but my brother ducked instead, and the ball went sailing over him and right into one of the jars of jam Granny had set on the fence to cool.

"Look what you did!" Pasha scolded.

"It wasn't my fault," my brother protested.

"Quiet," I said. "If Granny finds out, she'll kill us."

We all stood motionless, terrified, as if lost and waiting for something or someone to devour us. But nothing happened, and after a few minutes we simply moved to a different spot and continued to play. Eventually both Yura and I were hit, and it was our turn to throw the ball at Pasha and Anya. We obviously didn't move far enough away, because I was the next one to break a jar. It went crashing to the ground, and a warm strawberry smell wafted from the pool of fruit and glass. Again we all looked in the direction of the country house, but Granny and Grandpa must have been napping because we didn't hear a sound. We ended up breaking four jars that day. Even in the shade it was over 40°C, and the jam remained on the baked ground in sticky little puddles. I remembered the story where Baba Yaga cast a spell on a young boy so that he would turn into a goat if he drank from a puddle, and I thought of teasing Yura into drinking from one. Insects soon began consuming the fruit, however, and I quickly forgot about it. Later, when Yura and I were both soundly spanked by Granny's large, callused hands, all I could see were those ripe berries covered with flies and ants. I often pictured this even later, after the fall of the Soviet Union, when we still needed to stand in long lines for bread, and I was the one who had to do it. But then, playing vybivaly, we never bothered to clean up our mess or hide it from our grandparents. We never even bothered to stop and rest. We were having too much fun.

The River

The stories have been gone for a long time now. Someone tore open my rucksack as I tried to climb aboard the train to take them to Papa. It was during the Great Patriotic War, and the train was packed, people pushing their way in, crawling through the windows. I was young and much stronger than today, of course, but I was also alone; I didn't know his stories had been stolen until it was too late. The saddest part is that the notebooks they were in were probably burned for fuel, Uncle Vanya's intelligence and wit consumed even before the war consumed his body.

I only remember one, "The River." Uncle Vanya, in addition to being an artist, had traveled widely as a youth, to the far edges of the Soviet Union, the western deserts of the Turkmen SSR, the southern mountains of the Uzbek SSR, places where the chadra was still worn. Naturally, the authorities later corrected this, but the old Eastern ways persisted for a while. Uncle Vanya's story was about a girl who, while trying to cross a river to reach her village, fell into the deep, rushing waters. She became entangled in her chadra and drowned.

I always felt sorry for that girl, so weighted down by her society and her beliefs that it killed her. Uncle Vanya described it all so vividly. The chadra was light but long, some so long they dragged on the ground or billowed behind the women while they walked, which, I will admit, sounded beautiful. The top of the veil was like a knitted cap, snugly fitting, and the front panel hung over the face and shoulders. To see clearly through the mesh over the eyes, the women had to pull it close to them. Can you imagine that? That was when the men were around. By themselves or at home they simply tossed it back or let the folds drape around their faces, framing them very prettily. Even in the small mountain villages, they took care of their looks—washing their hair in yogurt, coloring their eyebrows and lids with usma to accent their dark eyes.

I can almost see her now, that beautiful drowned girl. She was carrying a bundle of firewood. Except for being Muslim and wearing the chadra, she was a lot like me. I was told I was quite beautiful when I was young, and I had to carry firewood, too. We were living in town then, and at night we had to steal fence posts, or the logs placed on the ground to walk on in winter. Had the authorities caught us, we would have been sent to prison. I didn't like breaking the law, but we needed the wood to stay alive. And I'd crossed mountain rivers, many of them, back when we lived in a village. Sometimes the water moves so quickly it can be frightening, and it's icy cold, even in summer, even far downstream from its source. How awful it would be to drown in such waters! I don't know what made Uncle Vanya think of such a story. He was a good man, someone who always did what he was told, but he was an artist. We all understood that and were protective of him, because we didn't want him to get into trouble. I understood his story, though it was strange and maybe even a little decadent. He captured so well the spirit of a bright old culture, if superstitious and backwards compared to the modern state we were building—how she carried firewood on her head, not over the shoulder in a strapped-up bundle like we did, how the silver bracelets jangled around her ankles as she moved along the mountain path.

She came to the river and stepped into it. It was cold, but she had crossed it hundreds of times in her life, and the rocky bottom felt familiar under her sandals. The water was higher than usual because of the spring thaw, but it was the river's narrowest and shallowest point for several kilometers, and, as Uncle Vanya wrote, she had done this hundreds of times. She moved slowly but surely.

The sun blazed overhead. The water was up to her knees, but she was strong, not like the girls living in the city today. Do you think they could or would carry firewood for kilometers like we used to, that Muslim girl and I? She's strong, and she moves steadily through the water, her chadra pulled downstream like a wildly wriggling snake that won't let go. There's the path again on the other shore, just two meters more.

Then she slips and falls. My heart always beats faster when I think of this. There's no reason; accidents just happen in life. She falls, and the rocks are slippery, and when she tries to get up, she's pushed downstream by the strong current. Today's girls wouldn't know what to do. They probably would try to call on their cell phones for their boyfriends to come and save them. But I was a strong swimmer, just like that Muslim girl. She begins swimming toward the shore. But the current has pushed her into a wider, deeper part of the river, and her chadra has become tightly curled around her body. Can you imagine how terrible that feels? She tries to sweep her arms in the broad arcs that will pull her to safety but instead finds herself in a tangle of cloth. The veil has wrapped itself about her neck; nearly everywhere she looks is darkness, only the faintest glimmering of sunlight through water through the small mesh opening. I was a strong swimmer, but what could I have done? The water is cold. The river is pulling everything downstream. Uncle Vanya, Papa, where are you? They say you're enemies of the people, but I know that's not true. I'm trying to swim, but my arms won't move. I'm swept into a big pool and pulled by the undertow to the very bottom. I can't see, so I pull the veil close, peer through the mesh. Nothing but white bubbles boiling all around. I don't know which way is up or down. I try to swim in any direction, but the undertow keeps me at the bottom. My limbs are growing cold. I've swallowed a lot of water, and my insides are cold. The darkness doesn't seem so scary now. I think I'll rest here for a while. The current gently tugs at my body, pushing it this way and that, like an Eastern dancer. The veil slowly unwinds, and I can see the pebbly riverbed clearly now, the big boulders along the sides, everything bathed in a soft light. The current folds the cloth around my face, framing it very prettily.

A Husband and Wife Are One Satan

Neither of them could remember exactly when their arguments began bringing more business to their café. A certain amount of public obnoxiousness could be expected in Kazakhstan, especially when vodka was involved, but normally the deeply personal affairs of a husband and wife were kept secret, behind the locked doors of crumbling Soviet-era apartments or closed gates of tiny village homes.

That doesn't mean people were above prying into their neighbors' lives, especially in the villages. Raim and Railya made it easy for them.

It started out playfully. "Mare," Raim would say, smacking his wife on her great round behind, which shivered like a horse's flank under her cotton skirt. "Stallion," she would return, grabbing him by his fleshy hips and then pushing him away, laughing.

The few customers who came at first, mostly their friends and relatives, enjoyed this little theater. Then one day Raim returned drunk from a trip to the bazaar to buy onions, and Railya soundly scolded him for "coming in on his eyebrows" in front of the entire café.

"You're really under her heel!" roared the big foundry boss, Kolya, and everybody laughed. Raim, normally good natured, and too drunk to fight back anyway, grinned sheepishly.

"But it's a very pretty heel," he said, trying to wink but blinking both eyes instead.

Once the taboo was broken, they began arguing as freely in their café as they did at home. Being ethnic Tatars, descendents of the Mongols who had ravaged the region some eight hundred years before, they already enjoyed a certain reputation for wildness. At some point they realized that business had become brisk. Just how much was due to their tasty homestyle cooking and how much to the entertainment was uncertain, but Railya shrewdly observed that there were certain phrases that always pleased her diners, who even insisted that the thunderous pop music, normally a café's main attraction, be turned down in order to hear what the combatants were saying.

It was a summer Friday night, and the regulars were all there: married, bear-like Kolya and his doll-like girlfriend, Larisa; Murat, a quiet little Kazakh man, and Tikhan, the equally quiet Russian youth who always sat with him; Dilya and Olya, excitable and extravagant teenage friends; and Alikhan, a widower everyone assumed was alcoholic because he strangely sat by himself and never spoke except to order.

Raim bustled between his roles of greeting customers, grilling large skewers of meat, and dishing out portions from a massive cauldron of plov—long-boiled rice, carrots, and onions topped with mutton.

"Assalamu alaikum," he greeted Murat as he did all his fellow Muslims: "Peace be with you."

"Wa alaikum assalam," Murat returned. They gripped hands lightly but warmly, their free hands holding each other's forearms to show respect.

Since Kolya was Christian, Raim greeted him in Russian and shook his hand in the vigorous Western style. In such a way Raim visited each table to ensure that his customers were happy. They all settled into their seats while Railya topped off everyone's glasses with their drinks of choice.

Then the show began.

"Your portions are too big," Railya complained, emphasizing each word by pointing a spoon nearly as large as a ladle at her husband. As a schoolgirl in Soviet times, she had often starred in the many holiday pageants the authorities staged, and she relished reliving the emotions of those days.

"People come here because they're hungry," Raim said. "I feed them."

"They'll have to feed us soon if you keep giving away everything we own."

"It might do you good to relax and open up a little, you dried-up old galosh."

"I gave you the best years of my life! If I'm dried-up, it's because you sucked me dry."

"Stop your talking, snake."

"Bloodsucker!"

"Stubborn ewe!"

"Deaf farter!" Her eyes twinkled, for she often used this epithet affectionately with him. "You're lucky I married you—you from a family of cattle thieves. I'm a head taller than you!"

Kolya began laughing so hard tears streamed down his ruddy cheeks. "That's exactly what my wife says!" he exclaimed between sobs before downing a shot of vodka. His girlfriend patted him consolingly on the arm. He placed his enormous free hand upon hers, and half her slender forearm disappeared.

*

They came for different reasons: Kolya to escape his wife, Larisa to be with Kolya, Dilya and Olya to find men, Murat and Tikhan to cure boredom, Alikhan to be alone in a crowd. Or so they thought. But had some sensitive soul come in, some spiritual master or poet, this soul would have felt them connected by a common energy, an energy unseen to them but to the spiritual master or poet as tangible as the blue-white glow simultaneously broadcasting the same flickering patterns from identical square boxes out window after window onto street after street night after night.

"We're already nineteen," Dilya lamented one night to her friend. "Do you think we'll ever get married?"

Both had broad, plain faces heavily made up, short, tight skirts pulled over wide hips, and large breasts barely harnessed in halter tops. They could have been sisters except that Dilya was ethnic Kazakh, with a dark complexion and long, black hair, Olya ethnic Russian, with a fair complexion and long, blonde hair.

"What about Timur?" Olya asked.

"He doesn't love me. He only thinks I'm pretty. I let him buy me presents."

"If he steals you, will you marry him?"

"Of course. I'm a good girl! I wouldn't disgrace my family. But," Dilya sighed, "he really is a bonehead."

"You would learn to love him."

"Yes, that's true. As God wishes. Mama was stolen by Papa, and they didn't love each other at first."

Dilya began looking around the room and quickly focused her attention on one table.

"What do you think of him?" she asked.

Olya glanced to where her friend seemed to be looking, then to the left, to the right, and back to her friend.

"Who?"

"Tikhan!"

Olya shrugged and then turned her attention to another table. "Kolya, though," she sighed. "Now there's a man!"

"What about Larisa?"

"Who cares about her, tiny little princess? I'd show Kolya what a real Russian woman is like."

"Olya, what are you saying?"

"After we're married, of course." She took a sip of beer. "I'm a good girl."

At the other table, as if he could sense that he was being overlooked again, Murat shifted self-consciously in his chair. Nobody could remember what he had done during Soviet times, and nobody knew exactly what he did today. Almost apologetically short, with elegant hands and glasses that made his eyes look like an owl's, he gave off the air of an academic in how he always ordered his food in perfect, precise Russian, the way he arranged his napkin neatly on his lap. In truth, he was a businessman involved in some shady dealings, as most even modestly successful businessmen in the country were, backing up his lack of physical stature with money.

Tikhan also appeared to be an academic and in fact had studied so well at the university that he hadn't needed to bribe his teachers for his good grades. Everyone assumed he now spent his days and nights in lofty intellectual pursuits, perhaps preparing for a master's program, but he actually spent much of his free time watching television. His favorite show was *The Big Wash*, which featured regular people talking about such themes as "I lived in America," "I want to be a star," and "I will never forget my wedding." Other guests listening in an adjacent room would then join, and arguments often ensued. He also liked *The Burden of Money*, where people competed for a fat cash award by telling a serious-faced "jury" their most sorrowful personal tales. Tikhan's main connection to Murat was that they both enjoyed drinking pot after pot of strong green tea with sugar.

At that moment, Tikhan caught the girls looking in his direction again, and they both immediately looked away and bent their heads together in conspiratorial giggles. At length they collapsed back in their chairs, two glorious fallen angels, spiritual emptiness radiating from them like halos.

*

A favorite crowd-pleaser at the café was any variation on the "I told you so" theme, usually with Raim ignoring the advice of his wife to his unacknowledged detriment.

"Look at this," Railya said, pointing to the empty cauldron with her ever-handy spoon. "Not only are your portions too big, I told you we didn't have enough rice."

"It was enough," he said meekly.

"Enough? Then why are our customers wanting for plov in the middle of lunch?"

"How should I know? Perhaps you ate some while I was at the bazaar."

"Do I look like I can eat that much?"

"When a man has a good woman, he wants a lot of her."

"Hornless devil!"

"At least you didn't give me horns," he asserted, for she had never cheated on him. Even Murat laughed merrily at this, and Kolya pounded the table with his great paw.

"Never," Railya responded with a frankness that seemed too frank in their little theater. "You may be an old tree stump, but I would never do that to you."

Raim was somewhat taken aback. "Is that a compliment or the truth?"

"It's the truth. You're an old tree stump."

Everyone laughed again, and Raim slipped comfortably back into the improvisation.

"A sore on your tongue!" he cried.

“You see?” she said. “You know that I’m right, so you have nothing but empty words.”

“Stop your nonsense.”

“Words, words, words.”

“Take yourself by the mind, woman.”

“Oh, this is better than *Windows*,” Larisa squealed happily. She loved the outrageous allegations people confronted one another with on this show. She especially loved the story—one she secretly considered trying out herself someday, though, of course, she would never tell Kolya—of the boyfriend who claimed to have caught his girlfriend making love to her sports bike. “Don’t you think so?”

Kolya nodded, vigorously stroking his long, bushy sideburns. Raim was staring steadily at his wife.

“Why are you looking at me like a goat at new gates?” she finally asked.

“A goat am I? Why are you so stubborn, like a ewe?”

“Goat!”

“Ewe!”

“Yes, yes!” Kolya cried. “This is life!”

*

Summer’s desert heat gave way to autumn’s coolness flowing down from the mountains, not like a flash flood but like the watery molecules that slowly saturate the air, then become dew on morning grass, then rain. The process is imperceptible day by day. In the same way, something changed in how Raim and Railya behaved.

One morning he came back from his trip to the bazaar without returning her greeting.

"Oh, did we sleep together?" she asked sarcastically.

"Hm?"

"A 'hello' for your wife would be nice."

"Hello, Dyuimovochka," he grunted distractedly. She understood this reference to the one-inch-tall fairytale girl, suggesting that she wasn't looking well—understood it as perfectly as the smell coming from his lips.

"Again you came in on your eyebrows!" she cried.

"Not in either eye," he snorted back, though he took care not to move too close to her.

"Let me take a look."

"I told you, there's nothing to see!" He busied himself with washing his hands in the corner washbasin, and when he turned back around, she was in the exact same position as before, hands on hips, reproach in her eyes.

"Why are you looking at me like Lenin at the bourgeoisie?" he spluttered. As they traded insults this time, their eyes remained hard.

"Deaf farter!"

"Old galosh!"

"Wood-goblin!"

"Witch!"

Eventually Alikhan caught Railya's attention and silently pointed to his empty shot glass.

*

A month later, everything appeared normal—Larisa picking her teeth while Kolya stroked her hair, Murat and Tikhan drowning themselves in tea and sugar, Dilya and Olya alternately whispering and giggling giddily over beers, Alikhan a sleepy-eyed statue over his vodka. But Railya sensed that something was different. When Raim returned from the bazaar this time, she instinctively pressed toward him to catch a whiff of the vodka she was certain was evaporating on his lips. She caught a whiff of something else instead. She recoiled as if he had smacked her forehead with a teakettle.

"Who is she?" she shouted.

"Who's who?" Raim returned, backing away.

"She, she, she! The whore whose perfume is all over your neck!"

"Perfume? That's not perfume. It's oil. I spilled some on myself when I was helping Baltibek fix his car."

"You spilled some on your neck? Why do you lie to me? Why do you protect that filthy bitch?"

He only stared at her, and with a sudden feeling of great fear, she softened.

"Raim," she pleaded, "please tell me it was just an accident, a little kiss, a one-time thing. Please tell me it was nothing."

Something about her fear and complete vulnerability annoyed and then angered him, bringing long-buried feelings to the surface, where they simmered, then boiled—an irrational stew of feelings that he could no longer contain.

"You drove me to this!" he shouted. "You want to know, yes? All the details? Okay. It's Gulshat, Baltibek's wife. We've been sleeping together for a month. There. Ever since we opened this café, you've grown colder and colder, and with your constant nagging, what else could I do? Maybe to you it was all a joke, but I'm a man, I have my pride. You—"

He cut himself short. His confession itself didn't startle the patrons of the café. A certain amount of infidelity was expected of men, even seen in the village as manly, and Gulshat had been the subject of certain rumors for some time. What startled them was that Raim had managed to keep it a secret until now.

Railya, however, was more than startled. She felt as if she had been cut with a knife—a real physical pain, searingly hot around the edges of the cut.

Her customers now experienced something they had almost forgotten about—silence. This silence settled deeply inside their souls as their busy minds stopped churning for a moment and they realized, startlingly, they were in a café with real bodies and feet connected to the floor. They moved uncomfortably in their seats, and to see Railya standing before them silent and cut made them more uncomfortable, and at that point they would have done anything to make the merry machinery they were accustomed to begin madly whirling again.

Raim felt the same way, and he instinctively put that machinery into motion.

"You drove me to this!" he repeated. "What was I supposed to do? What could I have done?"

Railya remained unmoving and silent.

"It was this, all this," he spluttered, spreading his hands before him, unsure of what to do or say next, his eyes sweeping the room from the lone tap of the single beer they sold to the cauldron of plov steaming over the fire. For a moment, he seemed mesmerized by the gleaming metal, the licking flames.

"I did it for our business!" he suddenly screeched. "Don't you understand? I did it for us!"

"You always gave away too much," she finally whispered.

For the first time anyone could remember, Alikhan said something other than to order food or drink.

"Pravda… pravda," he said, nodding emphatically: "Truth… truth."

*

In these times, Railya could have divorced him. However, for a traditional Tatar woman living in a village, the known world stopping at its boundary, not so much its physical boundary but the much stronger one of society and its mores, where would she have gone? And what could she have done? No one in her family had ever been divorced, and more importantly, they relied on her to help support them. For Raim and Railya, the café was their sole means of income, and one they managed themselves; they couldn't close it or take time off from work. So they moved into a nether world ruled by neither matter nor spirit. They continued to come day after day, more like memories of themselves than anything else, going through the motions of opening the shop, preparing the food, and serving their dwindling number of customers.

Autumn's fluid coolness gave way to winter's freezing snows, which blew down from the mountains and regularly, imperceptibly at first, added to what remained from before. In the same way, Raim brought bouquets of red roses whose petals over time withered and fell, softly, to the floor, gathering in drifts that neither Railya nor anyone else bothered to sweep up. After a while the café was filled with the frail, crushed scent of roses underfoot.

Raim hadn't touched a drop of alcohol since his confession and had even, in an entirely novel development for him, visited the mosque on a few occasions. He understood what he had done and felt sorry for it, but he also understood, with a knowledge that only could have come from some spontaneous and miraculous form of grace and certainly not from his own limited consciousness, that words were not needed—moreover, that spoken now they would permanently ruin everything between them. He continued to bring flowers and wait.

Then one day, which just happened to be a day when the regulars had all assembled for the first time since the confession, or perhaps exactly because of that, Raim decided to speak.

"Railya," he said softly, though it sounded like an explosion. "Dear."

She didn't turn to look at him, but she stopped preparing tea for Murat and Tikhan, her body tense, as if ready for flight.

Raim thought quickly but carefully. This new feeling in him was too fresh to trust to his own voice. As a Soviet schoolboy, he had been forced to memorize countless poems, many of which, all these years later, he could still remember. He searched his mind for his favorite poet, Pushkin, and for a verse that would appropriately reflect his feelings. He found one well known to everyone in the room:

I loved you: yet love may be
In my soul faded not completely.
But let it not disturb you again;
I do not wish to sadden you with anything.
I loved you silently, hopelessly,
Tormented now by timidity, now by jealousy;
I loved you so sincerely, so tenderly,
May God grant you such love from another.

He spoke slowly, simply. When he was done, he stood like a child at the head of the classroom, not knowing if he should say more or sit down.

"Perhaps..." he began and then stopped, for the thought was far too fragile and important to give words to.

Railya blinked, slowly, twice. Then, as if for the first time, she noticed all those petals on the floor. Mechanically she moved toward the broom, and when passing her husband, though she still didn't look at him, she spoke:

"Not yet," she said quietly. "But we will see."

Kolya's eyes began burning redly, and Larisa patted his arm.

"Two boots make a pair," she said.

Kolya hoisted a shot of vodka to his thick, moist lips and said to her, the whole room, and no one in particular, "A husband and wife are one Satan."

Znamenskaya Russkaya Pravoslavnaya Tserkov (The Holy Sign Russian Orthodox Church)

Gennady Nikolaevich Solovyov arrived earlier than usual before the service to perform his devotions. The old babushki, those who sold seeds to visitors wishing to feed the pigeons, were already taking their places. A new one had come today, and the others were arguing with her.

"You have your regular spot," said the large woman who always sat on the north bench. "Why don't you stay there?"

"This is God's place, not yours," the newcomer said. "Anyone can come here."

"There isn't enough room for us all."

"Not true. You eat honey by the spoonful, and we're living half-starved."

Though Gennady walked with a cane, he passed by quickly. A pensioner himself, he normally would have stopped and idly chatted for a while. But he had something important to pray about this morning, and he didn't want to waste a moment.

He had to be careful moving through the scaffolding in front of the main doorway. Far above him, workers were repainting the central onion dome in gold, one of the nearby lesser cupolas in bright swirls of pink, orange, green, and blue. One of the few reminders of tsarist times left in the city, the building had been turned back to the church only a decade ago, in 1995, and there was still much work to do, Gennady thought, still much work to do.

He took off his cap, folded it, and stuffed it into his jacket pocket before crossing himself and entering. Inside, old babushki dressed in black moved like careful ghosts in their eternal job of sweeping, mopping, dusting, polishing. He purchased a candle at the lavka in the vestibule and then walked into the dimly lit, incense-filled sanctuary. Ahead stood the beautiful and imposing iconostasis through which the priest would come to deliver the Divine Liturgy—the various rows depicting local saints, annual festivals, Old Testament prophets and patriarchs, and, in the very center, Christ as Judge of the world. Gennady turned right until he found the familiar icon of St. Nikolai, patron saint of Russia, where the Solovyov family had lived before being forced to immigrate to Kazakhstan, back when it was a Soviet republic.

St. Nikolai wore the traditional plain robe and stole of a Russian Orthodox priest. His right hand made the sign of blessing; his left held an open Bible inscribed with a verse from Matthew: *Ye are the salt of the earth: but if the salt have lost his savour, wherewith shall it be salted? It is thenceforth good for nothing, but to be cast out, and to be trodden under foot of men*. Though the icon's colors had darkened with age, the saint looked at him so lovingly, full of so many assurances, Gennady had to keep himself from crying. It was something he found himself doing more often in the past couple of years.

A bank of candles hissed and sparked, sending their attached prayers to heaven. Gennady carefully lit his own candle and placed it next to the others. He then crossed himself again and quietly prayed his morning prayer.

"...Suddenly the Judge shall come, and the deeds of each shall be laid bare; but with fear do we cry at midnight: Holy, Holy, Holy art Thou, O God; through the Mother of God, have mercy on us."

He had come to the end.

"Lord, have mercy," he prayed the first of twelve repetitions, "Lord, have mercy..."

The priest suddenly burst through the Holy Door in the

iconostasis and almost ran to meet the group of men who had entered.

"What do you want?" he demanded.

"What we want doesn't matter," said the one with small, dark eyes and high, pointed cheekbones. "The needs of the state are all that matter."

Three younger priests ran up to join the first, who was now gesturing angrily.

"Take off your hats. This is a house of God."

"God is dead. Or haven't you heard?"

"Blasphemer!" the head priest shouted. The small-eyed man lunged at him, and the two groups merged, the long, plain robes and stoles, the coarse shirts and trousers. The priests were big-boned and muscular, but there were too many against them, some with clubs.

"Superstitious fools," the small-eyed man muttered, wiping splatters of blood from his eyes.

The workers outside continued boarding up the building. They worked quickly, without care, driving in nails at wrong angles and occasionally shattering the few panes that remained in the windows. Dust shook down from the buttresses and rafters. Dust covered everything.

There's a name…

Gennady was sweating now. He made an invocation to his beloved patron:

"Pray unto God for me O holy God-pleaser, St. Nikolai, for I fervently flee unto thee, the speedy helper and intercessor for my soul."

He hesitated, stumbling over his own words. A black-clad babushka began sweeping in front of him, oblivious to his prayer.

"St. Nikolai, please help my grandson. He's sick, and the

doctors don't know what's wrong. I'm just an idler, a sinner, but you've always been good to our family. My father was named after you. I know you love the children. Please help him. He's a young boy, pure and unspoiled. I am weak; I am unworthy. I know I shouldn't have gone to that old Gypsy woman, but I'm here now. I'll make any offering you ask of me. Please tell me if it's true what she said."

A girl twirled in the hands of her partner, her skirt flaring and falling over her smooth calves. He smartly led, only the faintest perspiration beading on his thinly mustached lip. When the orchestra finished playing, the couple joined the other dancers in enthusiastic applause.

"This is wonderful!" the girl exclaimed. She began walking toward the row of chairs along the wall. "Imagine, my grandmother says this used to be a church."

He looked at the fresh white plastering, the bright new electric chandelier, and shrugged.

"It's the Culture Palace of the Metallurgical Plant now."

She suddenly bent forward and started coughing.

"Sweetheart, what's wrong?" he asked, but she couldn't answer. She couldn't stop coughing.

Outside a crash followed by lusty shouting as the cross atop the bell tower was pulled down.

There's a name for those like you…

Gennady was oblivious to these vibrations around him, tasteless salt under his thick-soled shoes. O holy God-pleaser, can you answer the prayers deepest in a man's heart, so deep even memory of them was lost long ago? Can you even hear these prayers? Lord, have mercy! Lord, have mercy…

A roan stallion limped in, a deep bloody cut on its foreleg. A man led it to a stall near the back, where another man was administering a shot to a sorrel mare.

"What happened?"

"White partisans."

The second man finished his job and then looked closely at the stallion's leg. The smell of incense hung in the air.

"This one will have to be put down. Make sure you collect every scrap of meat."

"…an idler… a sinner…"

It was because of something he'd done that his grandson was sick; he knew it. He didn't know what, but his grandson was sick.

"Where superstition once ruled, reason is now on display for all to see."

The director proudly led a group of officials toward the two large east apses. One had been converted into a gallery. Its neighbor held a small library.

"Welcome to the first museum to atheism in the city," he said.

Gennady was praying so fervently that sweat dripped from his white eyebrows and the end of his red nose.

"O holy God-pleaser, please. I'm an idler and a sinner, but I know you love the children."

The unspoken prayers deep inside him gave flesh to the ghosts around him, and they pressed closer, muttering more loudly, insistently. There's a name for those like you—watchers who do nothing, or who turn away without watching, listeners who keep silent. Do you know what it is? He tried to remember what he had done. Eighty-seven years old, electrical engineer, infantry in the Great Patriotic War, wife, six grown children… six, and three… three… trodden underfoot by the state. They were just children. Lord have mercy! And there it was, though he tried to push it down, that name, that awful burden, ever thirsty for a shot or a bottle, invoker of strange soul whispers and restless dreams.

Christ as Judge of the world could hardly bestow a more terrible title for the damned: Survivor.

He suddenly opened his eyes. He could see nothing—neither the old babushka sweeping in front of him nor the bank of candles that had all flickered out, nothing in his whole life or the history of this church. All his years of living and the times in which he had lived them had given him nothing. He felt such a terror at this that he couldn't stop trembling.

The girl in the flowing skirt couldn't stop coughing while members of the orchestra went in search of vodka. A horse whinnied, and another responded. Nails were being pulled out; nails were being pounded in.

The entire time, St. Nikolai held his right hand, unwavering, above Gennady's head. Slowly his vision returned. Tears streamed down his soft, broad cheeks. He reached out for that face, that loving, reassuring face, and though it was only half a meter away, he might have been reaching across the space of a hundred years, a thousand, reaching, reaching, reaching . . .

Acknowledgments

Bayou Magazine: "Learning to Fly at the End of an Empire"

Crab Orchard Review: "The River"

Fjords Review: "Znamenskaya Russkaya Pravoslavnaya Tserkov (The Holy Sign Russian Orthodox Church)"

Potomac Review: "A Husband and Wife Are One Satan"

Rosebud Magazine: "Accomplices to a Tradition"

"Accomplices to a Tradition" and "A Husband and Wife Are One Satan" were later selected for inclusion in the anthologies *Out of Many: Multiplicity and Divisions in America Today* (Cat in the Sun Press) and *Everywhere Stories: Short Fiction from a Small Planet* (Press 53), respectively. The latter story additionally won the Mary Mackey Short Story Prize from the National League of American Pen Women.

I also wish to thank my colleagues and critical readers par excellence Joshua Lamb and the late Dr. Richard Spear, Orison Books founder/editor Luke Hankins, and designer Alyssa Barnes. Finally, heartfelt thanks to my wife Valentina, for everything. The poem by Pushkin included in the title story and the Platonov quote were translated by Valentina and myself.

About the Author

Jeff Fearnside is the author of two full-length books, the short story collection *Making Love While Levitating Three Feet in the Air* (Stephen F. Austin State University Press) and the essay collection *Ships in the Desert* (forthcoming from the SFWP Press). His work has appeared widely in literary journals such as *The Paris Review*, *Los Angeles Review*, *Story*, *The Pinch*, and *The Sun*. Awards for his writing include a Grand Prize in the Santa Fe Writers Project's Literary Awards Program, the Mary Mackey Short Story Prize, and an Individual Artist Fellowship award from the Oregon Arts Commission. Fearnside lived in Central Asia for four years and has taught writing and literature at the Academy of Languages in Kazakhstan and various institutions in the U.S.

About Orison Books

Orison Books is a 501(c)3 non-profit literary press focused on the life of the spirit from a broad and inclusive range of perspectives. We seek to publish books of exceptional poetry, fiction, and non-fiction from perspectives spanning the spectrum of spiritual and religious thought, ethnicity, gender identity, and sexual orientation.

As a non-profit literary press, Orison Books depends on the support of donors. To find out more about our mission and our books, or to make a donation, please visit www.orisonbooks.com.

For information about supporting upcoming Orison Books titles, please visit www.orisonbooks.com/donate, or write to Luke Hankins at editor@orisonbooks.com.